Mr Wrong

Elizabeth Jane Howard

A Phoenix Paperback

Mr Wrong first published by Jonathan Cape Ltd in 1975

This edition published in 1996 by Phoenix
a division of Orion Books Ltd
Orion House, 5 Upper St Martin's Lane, London WC2H 9EA

Copyright © Elizabeth Jane Howard 1975

ISBN 1 85799 762 X

Typeset by Deltatype Ltd, Ellesmere Port, Cheshire
Printed in Great Britain by Clays Ltd, St Ives plc

Mr Wrong

Everybody – that is to say the two or three people she knew in London – told Meg that she had been very lucky indeed to find a car barely three years old, in such good condition and at such a price. She believed them gladly, because actually buying the car had been the most nerve-racking experience. Of course she had been told – and many times by her father – that all car dealers were liars and thieves. Indeed, to listen to old Dr Crosbie, you would think that nobody could *ever* buy a second-hand car, possibly even any *new* car, without its brakes or steering giving way the moment you were out of sight of the garage. But her father had always been of a nervous disposition: and as he intensely disliked going anywhere, and had now reached an age where he could fully indulge this disapprobation, it was not necessary to take much notice of him. For at least fifteen of her twenty-seven years Meg silently put up with his saying that there was no place like home, until, certain that she had exhausted all the possibilities of the small market town near where they lived, she had exclaimed, 'That's just it, Father! That's why I want to see somewhere else – *not* like it.'

Her mother, who had all the prosaic anxiety about her only child finding 'a really nice young man, Mr Right' that kind, anxious mothers tend to have – especially if their daughter can be admitted in the small hours to be 'not exactly a beauty' – smiled encouragingly at Meg and said, 'But Humphrey, dear, she will always be coming back to stay. She *knows* this is her home, but all young girls need a change.' (The young part of this had become emphasized as Meg plodded steadily through her twenties with not a romance in sight.)

So Meg had come to London, got a job in an antique shop in the New King's Road, and shared a two-room flat with two other girls in Fulham. One of them was a secretary, and the other a model: both were younger than Meg and ten times as self-assured; kind to her in an off-hand manner, but never becoming friends, nothing more than people she knew – like Mr Whitehorn, who ran the shop that she worked in. It was her mother who had given Meg three hundred pounds towards a car, as the train fares and subsequent taxis were proving beyond her means. She spent very little in London: she had bought one dress at Laura Ashley, but had no parties to go to in it, and lacked the insouciance to wear it to work. She lived off eggs done in various ways, and quantities of instant coffee – in the shop and in the flat. Her rent was comfortably modest by present-day standards, she walked to work, smoked very occasionally, and set her own hair. Her father had given her a hundred pounds when she was twenty-one: all of this had been invested, and to it she now added savings from her meagre salary and finally went off to one of London's northern suburbs to answer an advertisement about a second-hand MG.

The car dealer, whom she had imagined as some kind of tiger in a loud checked suit with whisky on his breath, had proved to be more of a wolf in a sheepskin car-coat – particularly when he smiled, which displayed a frightening number of teeth that seemed to stretch back in his raspberry mouth and down his throat with vulpine largesse. He smiled often, and Meg took to not looking at him whenever he began to do it. He took her out on a test drive: at first he drove, explaining all the advantages of the car while he did so, and then he suggested that she take over. This she did, driving very badly, with clashing of gears and stalling the engine in the most embarrassing places. 'I can see you've got the hang of it,' Mr Taunton said. 'It's always difficult driving a completely new car. But you'll find that she's most reliable: will start in all weather, economical on fuel, and needs the minimum of servicing.'

When Meg asked whether the car had ever had an accident, he began to smile, so she did not see his face when he replied that it hadn't been an accident, just a slight brush. 'The respray, which I expect you've noticed, was largely because the panel-work involved, and mind you, it *was* only panel-work, made us feel that it could do with a more cheerful colour. I always think aqua-blue is a nice colour for a ladies' car. And this is definitely a ladies' car.'

She felt his smile receding when she asked how many previous owners the car had had. He replied that it had been for a short time the property of some small firm that had since gone out of business. 'Only driven by one of the directors and his secretary.'

That sounded all right, thought Meg: but she was also thinking that for the price this was easily the best car she could hope for, and somehow, she felt, he knew that she knew she was going to buy it. His last words were: 'I hope you have many miles of motoring before you, madam.' The elongated grin began, and as it was for the last time, she watched him – trying to smile back – as the pointed teeth became steadily more exposed down his cavernous throat. She noticed then that his pale grey eyes very nearly met, but were narrowly saved from this by the bridge of his nose, which was long and thrusting, and almost made up for his having a mouth that had clearly been eaten away by his awful quantity of teeth. They had nothing going for each other beyond her buying and his selling a car.

Back in the showroom office, he sank into his huge moquette chair and said: 'Bring us a coffee, duck. I've earned it.' And a moony-faced blonde in a mini-skirt with huge legs that seemed tortured by her tights, smiled and went.

Meg drove the MG – her *car* – back to London in the first state of elation she had ever known since she had won the bending competition in a local gymkhana. She had a car! Neither Samantha nor Val were in such a position. She really drove quite well, as she had had a temporary job working for a doctor near home who had lost his licence for two years. Away from Mr Taunton (*Clive* Taunton he had repeatedly said), she felt able and assured. The car was easy to drive, and responded, as MGs do, with a kind of husky excitement to speed.

When she reached the flat, Samantha and Val were so

impressed that they actually took her out to a Chinese meal with their two boy-friends. Meg got into her Laura Ashley dress and enjoyed every sweet and sour moment of it. Everybody was impressed by her, and this made her prettier. She got slightly drunk on rice wine and lager and went to work the next day, in her car, feeling much more like the sort of person she had expected to feel like in London. Her head ached, but she had something to show for it: one of the men had talked to her several times – asking where she lived and what her job was, and so forth.

Her first drive north was the following Friday. It was cold, a wet and dark night – in January she never finished at the shop in time even to start the journey in the light – and by the time she was out of the rush, through London and on Hendon Way, it was raining hard. She found the turn off to the M1 with no difficulty: only three hours of driving on that and then about twenty minutes home. It was nothing, really; it just seemed rather a long way at this point. She had drunk a cup of strong black instant at Mr Whitehorn's, who had kindly admired the car and also showed her the perfect place to park it every day, and she knew that her mother would be keeping something hot and home-made for her whatever time she got home. (Her father never ate anything after eight o'clock in the evening for fear of indigestion, something from which he had never in his life suffered and attributed entirely to this precaution.)

Traffic was fairly heavy, but it seemed to be more lorries than anything else, and Meg kept on the whole to the middle lane. She soon found, as motorists new to a motorway do, that the lanes, the headlights coming towards her, and the road glistening with rain had a hypnotic effect, as though she and the car had become minute, and she was being spun down some enormous, endless striped ribbon. 'I mustn't go to sleep,' she thought. Ordinary roads had too much going on in them for one to feel like that. About half her time up the motorway, she felt so tired with trying not to feel sleepy that she decided to stop in the next park, open the windows and have a cigarette. It was too wet to get out, but even stopping the windscreen-wipers for a few minutes would make a change. She stopped the engine, opened her window, and before she had time to think about smoking again, fell asleep.

She awoke very suddenly with a feeling of extreme fear. It was not from a dream; she was sitting in the driver's seat, cramped, and with rain blowing in through the open window, but something else was very wrong. A sound – or noises, alarming in themselves, but, in her circumstances, frighteningly out of place. She shut her window except for an inch at the top. This made things worse. What sounded like heavy, laboured, stertorous, even painful breathing was coming, she quickly realized, from the *back* of the car. The moment she switched on the car light and turned round, there was utter silence, as sudden as the noise stopping in the middle of a breath. There was nobody in the back of the car, but the doors were not locked, and her large carrier bag – her luggage – had fallen to the floor. She locked both doors, switched off the car light and the sounds began again, exactly where they had left off – in the middle of a breath. She put both the car light and her headlights on, and looked again in the back. Silence, and it was still empty. She considered making sure that there was nobody parked behind her, but somehow she didn't want to do that. She switched on the engine and started it. Her main feeling was to get away from the place as quickly as possible. But even when she had started to do this and found herself trying to turn the sounds she had heard into something else and accountable, they wouldn't. They remained in her mind, and she could all too clearly recall them, as the heavy breaths of someone either mortally ill, or in pain, or both, coming quite distinctly from the back of the car. She drove home as fast as she could, counting the minutes and the miles to keep her mind quiet.

She reached home – a stone and slate-roofed cottage – at a quarter past nine, and her mother's first exclamation when she saw her daughter was that she looked dreadfully tired. Instantly, Meg began to feel better; it was what her mother had always said if Meg ever did anything for very long away from home. Her father had gone to bed: so she sat eating her supper with surprising hunger, in the kitchen, and telling her mother the week's news about her job and the two girls she shared with and the Chinese-meal party. 'And is the car nice, darling?' her mother asked at length. Meg started to speak, checked herself, and began again. 'Very nice. It was so kind of you to give me all that money for it,' she said.

The weekend passed with almost comforting dullness, and Meg did not begin to dread returning until after lunch on Sunday. She began to say that she ought to pack; her mother said she must have tea before she left, and her father said that he didn't think that *anyone* should drive in the dark. Or, indeed, at all, he overrode them as they both started saying that it was dark by four anyway. Meg eventually decided to have a short sleep after lunch, drink a cup of tea and then start the journey. 'If I eat one of Mummy's teas, I'll pass out in the car,' she said, and as she said 'pass out', she felt an instant, very small, ripple of fear.

Her mother woke her from a dreamless, refreshing sleep at four with a cup of dark, strong Indian tea and two Bourbon biscuits.

'I'm going to pack for you,' she said firmly. She had also unpacked, while Meg was finishing her supper on Friday night. 'I've never known such a hopeless packer. All your clothes were cramped up and crushed together as though someone had been stamping on them. Carrier bags,' she scolded, enjoying every minute; 'I'm lending you this nice little case that Auntie Phil left me.'

Meg lay warmly under the eiderdown in her own room watching her mother, who quite quickly switched from packing to why didn't Meg drink her tea while it was hot. 'I know your father won't drink anything until it's lukewarm, but thank goodness, you don't take after him. In that respect,' she ended loyally, but Meg knew that her mother missed her, and got tired and bored dealing with her father's ever-increasing regime of what was good or bad for him.

'Can I come next weekend?' she asked. Her mother rushed across the room and enfolded her.

'I should be most upset if you didn't,' she said, trying to make it sound like a joke.

When Meg left, and not until she was out of sight of home, she began to worry about what had happened on the journey up. Perhaps it could have been some kind of freak wind, with the car window open, she thought. Being able even to think that encouraged her. It was only raining in fits and starts on the way back, and the journey passed without incident of any kind. By the time Meg had parked, and slipped quietly into the flat that turned out to be empty – both girls were out – she really began to imagine that she had imagined it. She ate a boiled egg, watched a short feature on Samantha's television about Martinique, and went to bed.

The following weekend was also wet, but foggy as well. At one moment during a tedious day in the shop (where there was either absolutely nothing to do, or an endless chore, like packing china and glass to go abroad), Meg thought of putting off going to her parents: but they were not on the telephone, and that meant that they would have to endure a telegram. She thought of her father, and decided against that. He would talk about it for six months, stressing it as an instance of youthful extravagance, reiterating the war that it had made upon his nerves, and the proof it was that she should never have gone to London at all. No – telegrams were out, except in an emergency. She would just have to go – whatever the weather, or anything else.

Friday passed tediously: her job was that of packing up the separate pieces of a pair of giant chandeliers in pieces of old newspaper and listing what she packed. Sometimes she got so bored by this that she even read bits from the old, yellowing newsprint. There were pages in one paper of pictures of a Miss World competition: every girl was in a bathing-dress and high-heeled shoes, smiling that extraordinary smile of glazed triumph. They must have an awfully difficult time, Meg thought – fighting off admirers. She wondered just how difficult that would turn out to be. It would probably get easier with practice.

At half past four, Mr Whitehorn let her go early: he was the kind of man who operated in bursts of absent-minded kindness, and he said that in view of her journey, the sooner she started the better. Meg drank her last cup of instant coffee, and set off.

Her progress through London was slow, but eventually she reached Hendon Way. Here, too, there were long hold-ups as cars queued at signal lights. There were also straggling lines of people trying to get lifts. She drove past a good many of these, feeling her familiar feelings about them, so mixed that they cancelled one another out, and she never, in fact, did anything about the hitchers. Meg was naturally a kind person: this part of her made her feel sorry for the wretched creatures, cold, wet, and probably tired; wondering whether they would *ever* get to where they wanted to be. But her father had always told her never to give lifts, hinting darkly at the gothic horrors that lay in wait for anyone who ever did that. It was not that Meg ever consciously agreed with her father; rather that in all the years of varying warnings, some of his anxiety had brushed off on her – making her shy, unsure of what to do about things, and feeling ashamed of feeling like that. No, she was certainly not going to give anyone a lift.

She drove steadily on through the driving sleet, pretending that the back of her car was full of pieces of priceless chandeliers, and this served her very well until she came to the inevitable hold-up before she reached Hendon, when a strange thing happened.

After moving a few yards forwards between each set of green lights, she finally found herself just having missed another lot, but head of the queue in the right-hand lane. There, standing under one of the tall, yellow lights, on an island in the streaming rain, was a girl. There was nothing in the least remarkable about her appearance at first glance: she was short, rather dumpy, wearing what looked like a very thin mackintosh and unsuitable shoes; her head was bare; she wore glasses. She looked wet through, cold and exhausted, but above all there was an air of extreme desolation about her, as though she was hopelessly lost and solitary. Meg found, without having thought at all about it, that she was opening her window and beckoning the girl towards the car. The girl responded – she was only a few yards away – and as she came nearer, Meg noticed two other things about her. The first was that she was astonishingly pale – despite the fact that she had dark, reddish hair and was obviously frozen: her face was actually livid, and when she extended a tentative hand in a gesture that was either seeking reassurance about help, or anticipating the opening of the car door, the collar of her mackintosh moved, and Meg saw that, at the bottom of her white throat, the girl had what looked like the most unfortunate purple birth mark.

'Please get in,' Meg said, and leaned over to open the seat beside her. Then two things happened at once. The girl simply got into the back of the car – Meg heard her open the door and shut it gently, and a man, wearing a large, check overcoat, tinted glasses and a soft black hat tilted over his forehead slid into the seat beside her.

14   'How kind,' he said, in a reedy, pedagogic voice

(almost as though he was practising to be someone else, Meg thought); 'we were wondering whether anyone at all would come to our aid, and it proves that charming young women like yourself behave as they appear. The good Samaritan is invariably feminine these days.'

Meg, who had taken the most instant dislike to him of anyone she had ever met in life, said nothing at all. Then, beginning to feel bad about this, at least from the silent girl's point of view, she asked:

'How far are you going?'

'Ah, now that will surprise you. My secretary and I broke down this morning on our way up, or down to Town,' he sniggered; 'and it is imperative that we present ourselves in the right place at the right time this evening. I only wish to go so far as to pick up our car, which should now be ready.' His breath smelled horribly of stale smoke and peppermints.

'At a garage?' The whole thing sounded to Meg like the most preposterous story.

'Between Northampton and Leicester. I shall easily be able to point the turning out to you.'

Again, Meg said nothing, hoping that this would put a stop to his irritating voice. 'What a bore,' she thought: 'I *would* be lumbered with this lot.' She began to consider the social hazards of giving people lifts. Either they sat in total silence – like the girl in the back – or they talked. At this point he began again.

'It is most courageous of you to have stopped. There are so many hooligans about, that I always say it is most unjust to the older and more respectable people. But it is true that an old friend of mine once gave a lift to a *young man*, and the next thing she knew, the poor dear was in a ditch; no car, a dreadful headache, and no idea where she was. It's perfectly ghastly what some people will do to some people. Have you noticed it? But I imagine you are too young: you are probably in search of *adventure – romance* – or whatever lies behind those euphemisms. Am I right?'

Meg, feeling desperately that *anything* would be better than this talking all the time, said over her shoulder to her obstinately silent passenger in the back: 'Are you warm enough?'

But before anyone else could have said anything, the horrible man said at once: 'Perfectly, thank you. Physically speaking, I am not subject to great sensitivity about temperature.' When he turned to her, as he always seemed to do, at the end of any passage or remark, the smell of his breath seemed to fill the car. It was not simply smoke and peppermints – underneath that was a smell like rotting mushrooms. 'She must be asleep,' Meg thought, almost resentfully – after all there was no escape for *her* – *she* could not sleep, was forced to drive and drive and listen to this revolting front-seat passenger.

'Plastic,' he continued ruminatively (as though she had even *mentioned* the stuff), 'the only real use that plastic has been to society was when the remains, but unmistakable – unlike the unfortunate lady – when the remains of Mrs Durand Deacon's red plastic handbag were discovered in the tank full of acid. Poor Haigh must have thought he was perfectly safe with acid, but of course, he had not reckoned on the durable properties of some plastics. That was the end of *him*. Are you familiar with the case at all?'

'I'm not very interested in murder, I'm afraid.'

'Ah – but fear and murder go hand in hand,' he said at once, and, she felt, deliberately misunderstanding her. She had made the mistake of apologizing for her lack of interest –

'. . . in fact, it would be difficult to think of any murder where there had not been a modicum, and sometimes, let's face it, a very great deal of fear.' Glancing at him, she saw that his face, an unhealthy colour, or perhaps that was the headlights of oncoming cars, was sweating. It could not still be rain: the car heater was on: it was sweat.

She stuck it out until they were well on the way up the M1. His conversation was both nasty and repetitive, or rather, given that he was determined to talk about fear and murder, he displayed a startling knowledge of different and horrible cases. Eventually, he asked suddenly whether she would stop for him, 'a need of nature', he was sure she would understand what he meant. Just there a lorry was parked on the shoulder, and he protested that he would rather go on – he was easily embarrassed and preferred complete privacy. Grimly, Meg parked.

'That will do perfectly well,' she said as firmly as she could, but her voice came out trembling with strain.

The man slid out of the car with the same reptilian action she had noticed when he got in. He did not reply. The moment that he was out, Meg said to the girl: 'Look here, if he's hitching lifts with you, I do think you might help a bit with the conversation.'

There was no reply. Meg, turning to the back, began almost angrily: 'I don't care if you are asleep –' but then she had to stop because a small scream seemed to have risen in her throat to check her.

The back seat was empty.

18   Meg immediately looked to see whether the girl could

have fallen off the back seat on to the floor. She hadn't. Meg switched on the car light; the empty black mock-leather seat glistened with emptiness. For a split second, Meg thought she might be going mad. Her first sight of the girl, standing under a lamp on the island at Hendon, recurred sharply. The pale, thin mac, the pallor, the feeling that she was so desolate that Meg had *had* to stop for her. But she had *got into* the car – of course she had! Then she must have got out, when the man got out. But he hadn't shut his door, and there had been no noise from the back. She looked at the back doors. They were both unlocked. She put out her hand to touch the seat: it was perfectly dry, and that poor girl had been so soaked when she had got in – *had got in* – she was certain of it, that if she had *just* got out, the seat would have been at least damp. Meg could hear her heart thudding now, and for a moment, until he returned, she was almost glad that even that man was some sort of company in this situation.

He seemed to take his time about getting back into the car: she saw him – as she put it – slithering out of the dark towards her, but then he seemed to hesitate; he disappeared from sight, and it was only when she saw him by the light of her right-hand side light that she realized he had been walking round the car. *Strolling* about, as though she was simply a chauffeur to him! She called through the window to him to hurry up, and almost before he had got into the car, she said, 'What on earth's become of your secretary?'

There was a slight pause, then he turned to her: 'My *secretary*?' His face was impassive to the point of offensiveness, but she noticed that he was sweating again.

'You know,' she said impatiently; she had started the engine and was pulling away from the shoulder: 'The girl you said you'd had a breakdown with on your way to London.'

'Ah yes: poor little Muriel. I had quite forgotten her. I imagine her stuffing herself with family high tea and, I don't doubt, boy-friend – some provincial hairdresser who looks like a pop star, or perhaps some footballer who looks like a hairdresser.'

'What *do* you mean?'

He sniggered. 'I am not given to oversight into the affairs of any employee I may indulge in. I do not like prolonged relationships of any kind. I like them sudden – short – and sweet. In fact, I –'

'No – *listen!* You know perfectly well what I'm talking about.'

She felt him stiffen, become still with wariness. Then,

quite unexpectedly, he asked: 'How long have you had this car?'

'Oh – a week or so. Don't make things up about your secretary. It was her I really stopped for. I didn't even see you.'

It must be his sweat that was making the car smell so much worse. 'Of course, I noticed at once that it was an MG,' he said.

'The girl in the back,' Meg said desperately: he seemed to be deliberately stupid as well as nasty. 'She was standing on the island, under a lamp. She wore a mac, but she was obviously soaked to the skin, I beckoned to her, and she came up and got into the back without a word. At the same time as you. So come off it, inventing nasty, sneering lies about your secretary. Don't pretend *you* didn't know she was there. You probably used her as a decoy – to get a lift at all.'

There was a short, very unpleasant silence. Meg was just beginning to be frightened, when he said, 'What did your friend look like?'

It was no use quibbling with him about not being the girl's friend. Meg said: 'I told you . . .' and instantly realized that she had done nothing of the kind. Perhaps the girl really hadn't been his secretary . . .

'All you have done is allege that you picked up my 21

secretary with me.'

'All right. Well, she was short – she wore a pale mac – I told you that – and, and glasses – her hair was a dark reddish colour – I suppose darker because she was wet through, and she had some silly shoes on and she looked *ill*, she was so white – a sort of livid white, and when she –'

'Never heard of her – never heard of anyone like her.'

'No, but you *saw* her, didn't you? I'm sorry if I thought she was your secretary – the point is you saw her, didn't you? *Didn't* you?'

He began fumbling in his overcoat pocket, from which he eventually drew out a battered packet of sweets, the kind where each sweet is separately wrapped. He was so long getting a sweet out of the packet and then starting to peel off the sticky paper that she couldn't wait.

'Another thing. When she put out her arm to open the door, I saw her throat –'

His fingers stopped unwrapping the paper. She glanced at them: he had huge, ugly hands that looked the wrong scale beside the small sweet –

'She had a large sort of birth mark at the bottom of her throat, poor thing.'

He dropped the sweet: bent forward in the car to find

it. When, at last, he had done so, he put it straight into his mouth without attempting to get any more paper off. Briefly, the smell of peppermint dominated the other, less pleasant odours. Meg said, 'Of course, I don't suppose for a moment you could have seen *that*.'

Finally, he said: 'I cannot imagine who, or what, you are talking about. I didn't see any *girl* in the back of *your* car.'

'But there couldn't be someone in the back of my car without my knowing!'

There seemed to Meg to be something wrong about his behaviour. Not just that it was unpleasant; wrong in a different way; she felt that he knew perfectly well about the girl, but wouldn't admit it – to frighten her, she supposed.

'Do you mind if I smoke?'

He seemed to be very bad at lighting it. Two matches wavered out in his shaky hands before he got an evil-smelling fag going.

Meg, because she still felt a mixture of terror and confusion about what had or had not happened, decided to try being very reasonable with him.

'When you got into the car,' she began carefully, 'you kept saying "we" and talking about your secretary. *That's* why I thought she must be.'

'Must be what?'

A mechanical response; sort of playing-for-time stuff, Meg thought.

'You must excuse me, but I really don't know what you are talking about.'

'Well, I think you *do*. And before you can say "do what?" I mean *do* know what you are talking about.'

She felt, rather than saw him glance sharply at her, but she kept her eyes on the road.

Then he seemed to make up his mind. 'I have a suggestion to make. Supposing we stop at the next service area and you tell me all about everything? You have clearly got a great deal on your mind; in fact, you show distinct symptoms of being upset. Perhaps if we –'

'No thank you.' The idea of his being the slightest use to talk to was both nauseating and absurd. She heard him suck in his breath through his teeth with a small hissing sound: once more she found him reminding her of a snake. Meg hated snakes.

Then he began to fumble about again, to produce a torch and to ask for a map. After some ruminating aloud as to where they were, and indeed where his garage was likely to be, he suggested stopping again 'to give my, I fear, sadly weakened eyes an opportunity to discover my garage'.

Something woke up in Meg, an early warning or premonition of more, and different trouble. Garages were not marked on her map. She increased their speed, stayed in the middle lane until a service station that she had noticed marked earlier at half a mile away loomed and glittered in the wet darkness. She drove straight in and said:

'I don't like you very much. I'd rather you got out now.' Again she heard him suck his breath in through his teeth. The attendant had seen the car, and was slowly getting into his anorak to come out to them.

'How cruel!' he said, but she sensed his anger. 'What a pity! What a chance lost!'

'Please get out at once, or I'll get the man to turn you out.'

With his usual agility, he opened the door at once, and slithered out.

'I'm sorry,' Meg said weakly: 'I'm sure you did know about the girl. I just don't trust you.'

He poked his head in through the window. 'I'm far from sure that I trust you.' There were little bits of scum at the ends of his mouth. 'I really feel that you oughtn't to drive alone if you are subject to such extreme hallucinations.'

There was no mistaking the malice in his voice, and

just as Meg was going to have one last go at his admitting that he *had* seen the girl, the petrol attendant finally reached her and began unscrewing her petrol cap. He went, then. Simply withdrew his head, as though there were not more of him than that, and disappeared.

'How many?'

'Just two, please.'

When the man went off slowly to get change, Meg wanted to cry. Instead, she locked all the doors and wound up the passenger window. She had an unreasonable fear that he would come back and that the attendant might not help her to oust him. She even forgot the change, and wound up her own window, so that nobody could get into the car. This made the attendant tap on her window; she started violently, which set her shivering.

'Did you – did you see where the man who was in the front of my car went. He got out just now.'

'I didn't see anyone. Anyone at all.'

'Oh thank you.'

'Night.' He went thankfully back to his brightly lit and doubtless scorching booth.

Before she drove off, Meg looked once more at the back seat. There was no one there. The whole experience had been so prolonged, as well as unnerving, that apart from feeling frightened she felt confused. She wanted badly to get away as fast as possible, and she wanted to keep quite still and try to sort things out. He *had* known that the girl had been in the car. He had enjoyed – her fear. Why else would he have said 'we' so much? This made her more frightened, and her mind suddenly changed sides.

The girl *could not* have got out of the back without opening and shutting – however quietly – the door. There had been no sound or sounds like that. In fact, from the moment the girl had got into the car she had made no sound at all. Perhaps she, too, had been frightened by the horrible man. Perhaps she had *pretended* to get in, and at the last moment, slipped out again.

She opened her window wide to get rid of the smells in the car. As she did so, a possible implication of what the petrol attendant had said occurred. He hadn't seen *anyone*; he hadn't emphasized it like that, but he had repeated 'anyone at all'. Had he just meant that he hadn't looked? Or had he looked, and seen nobody? Ghosts don't talk, she reminded herself, and at once was back to the utterly silent girl.

Her first journey north in the car, and the awful breathing sounds coming from its back, could no longer be pushed out of her mind. The moment that she realized this, both journeys pounced forward into incomprehensible close-ups of disconnected pictures and sounds, recurring more and more rapidly, but in different sequences, as though, through their speed and volume, they were trying to force her to understand them. In the end, she actually cried out: 'All *right*! The car is haunted. Of course, I see that!'

A sudden calm descended upon her, and in order to further it, or at least stop it as suddenly stopping, she added: 'I'll think about it when I get home,' and drove mindlessly the rest of the way. If any spasm about what had recently happened attempted to invade her essential blankness, she concentrated upon seeing her mother's face, smelling the dinner in the kitchen, and hearing her father call out who was there.

'. . . thought he might be getting a severe cold, so he's off to bed. He's had his arrowroot with a spot of whisky in it and asked us to be extra quiet in *case* he gets a wink of sleep.'

Meg hugged her without replying: it was no good trying to be conspiratorial with her mother about her father; there could never be a wink or a smile. Her mother's loyalty had stiffened over the years, until now she could relate the most absurd details of her father's imaginary fears and ailments with a good-natured but completely impassive air. 'Have we got anything to drink?' she asked.

'Darling – I'm sure we have somewhere. But it's so unlike you to want a drink that I didn't put it out. It'll be in the corner cupboard in the sitting-room.'

Meg knew this, knew also that she would find the untouched half-bottles of gin and Bristol Milk that were kept in case anyone 'popped in'. But the very few people who did always came for cups of tea or coffee at the appropriate times of day. Her parents could not really afford drink – except for her father's medicinal whisky.

When she brought the bottles into the kitchen, she said, 'You have one too. I shall feel depraved drinking all by myself.'

'Well dear, then I'll be depraved with you. Just a drop of sherry. We needn't tell Father. It might start him worrying about your London Life. Been meeting anyone interesting lately?'

Meg had offered her mother a cigarette with her sherry, and her mother, delighted, had nearly burned her wispy fringe bending over the match to light it, and was now blowing out frantic streams of smoke from her nose before it got too far. It was all right to smoke if you

29

didn't inhale. On a social occasion, that was. Like it being all right to drink a glass of sherry at those times.

'This *is* nice,' her mother said, and then added, 'Have you been *meeting* anyone nice, dear? At all your parties and things?'

It was then that Meg realized that she could not possibly – ever – pour out all her anxieties to her mother. Her mother simply would not be able to understand them. 'Not this week,' she said. Her mother sighed, but Meg was not meant to hear, and said that she supposed it took time in a place like London to know people.

Meg had a second, strong gin, and then said that she would pay her mother back, but she was tired, and needed a couple of drinks. She also smoked four cigarettes before dinner, and felt so revived that she was able to eat the delicious steak-and-kidney pie followed by baked apples with raisins in them. Her mother had been making Meg Viyella nightgowns with white lace ruffles, and wanted to show them to her. They were brought into the kitchen, which was used for almost everything in winter as it saved fuel. 'I've been quite excited about them,' her mother said, when she laid out the nightgowns. 'Not quite finished, but such fun doing each one in a different colour.'

She listened avidly when Meg told her things about

Mr Whitehorn and the shop: she even liked being told about the *things* in the shop. She laughed at Meg's descriptions when they were meant to be in the least amusing, and looked extremely earnest and anxious when Meg told her about the fragility and value of the chandeliers. When it was time to go to bed, and she had filled their two hot-water bottles, she accompanied Meg to the door of her bedroom. They kissed, and her mother said: 'Bless you, dearie. I don't know what I'd do without you. Although, of course, one of these days I shall have to when Mr Right comes along.'

Meg cleaned her teeth in the ferociously cold bath-room and went back to her – nearly as cold – bedroom. Hot-water bottles were essential: Viyella nightdresses would be an extra comfort. From years of practice, she undressed fast and ingeniously, so that at no time was she ever naked. Whenever her mother mentioned Mr Right she had a vision of a man with moustaches and wearing a bowler hat mowing a lawn. She said her prayers kneeling beside her high, rather uncomfortable bed, and the hot-water bottle was like a reward.

In the night she awoke once, her body tense and crowded with fears: 'I could *sell* the car, and get another,' she said, and almost at once relaxed, the fears receded until they fell through some blank slot at the back of her mind and she was again asleep.

This decision, combined with a weekend of comfortingly the same ordered, dull events made her able to set aside, almost to shut up, the things – as she called them – that had happened, or seemed to have happened, in the car. On Sunday morning she found her mother packing the back with some everlasting flowers 'for your flat', a huge dark old tartan car-rug 'in case you haven't enough on your bed', and a pottery jar full of home-made marmalade 'to share with your friends at breakfast'.

'There's plenty of room for the things on the floor, as you're so small, really, that you have your driving seat pushed right forward.'

When she said good-bye and set off, it was with the expectation of the journey to London being uneventful, and it was.

The trouble, she discovered, after trying in her spare time for a week, was that she *could not* sell the car. She had started with the original dealer who had sold it to her, but he had said, with a bland lack of regret, that he was extremely sorry, but this was not the time of year to sell second-hand cars and that the best he could offer was to take it back for a hundred pounds less than she had paid for it. As this would completely rule out having any other car excepting a smashed-up or clapped-out Mini that would land her with all kinds of garage bills (and, like most car-owners, Meg was not mechanically minded), she had to give up that idea from the start.

She advertised in her local newspaper shop (cheap, and it would be easy for people to try out the car) but this only got her one reply: a middle-aged lady with a middle-aged poodle who came round one evening. At first it seemed hopeful; the lady said it was a nice colour and looked in good condition, but when she got into the driver's seat with Meg beside her to drive it round the block, her dog absolutely refused to get into the back as he was told to do. His owner tried coaxing, and he whimpered and scrabbled out of the still-open door; she tried a very unconvincing authority: 'Cherry! Do as you are told at once,' and his whimpering turned to a series of squealing yelps. 'He *loves* going in cars. I don't know what's come over him!'

Out in the street again, all three of them, he growled and tried to snap at Meg. 'I'm sorry dear, but I can't possibly buy a car that Cherry won't go in. He's all I've got. Naughty Cherry. He's usually such a mild, sweet dog. Don't you dare bite at Mummy's friends.'

And that was that. She asked Mr Whitehorn and her flat-mates, and finally, their friends, but nobody seemed to want to buy her car, or even wanted to help her get rid of it. By Friday, Meg was in a panic at the prospect of driving north again in it. She had promised herself that she wasn't going to, and as long as the promise had seemed to hold (surely she could find *someone* who would want it) she had been able not to think about the alternative. By Friday morning she was so terrified that she did actually send a telegram to her mother, saying that she had 'flu and couldn't drive home.

After she had sent it, she felt guilty and relieved in about equal proportions. The only way she could justify such behaviour was to make sure of selling the car that weekend. Samantha told her to put in an ad in the *Standard* for the next day. 'You're bound to make the last edition anyway,' she said. So Meg rang them, having spent an arduous half-hour trying to phrase the advertisement. 'Pale blue MG –' was how it finally began.

Then she had to go to work. Mr Whitehorn was in one of his states. It was not rude to think this, since he frequently referred to them. There was a huge order to be sent to New York that would require, he thought, at least a week's packing. He had got hold of tea chests, only to be told that he had to have proper packing cases. 34 There was plenty of newspaper and straw in the basement. He was afraid that that was where Meg would have to spend her day.

The basement was whitewashed and usually contained only inferior pieces, or things that needed repair. While working, Meg was allowed to have an oil stove, but it was considered too dangerous to leave it on by itself. Her first job was a huge breakfast, lunch, tea and coffee service bought by Mr Whitehorn in a particularly successful summer sale in Suffolk. It had to be packed and listed, all two hundred and thirty-six pieces of it. It was lying on an old billiard table with a cut cloth, and Meg found that the most comfortable way to pack it was to bring each piece to a chaise-longue whose stuffing was bristling out at every point, and put the heap of newspapers on the floor beside her. Thus she could sit and pack, and after each section of the set she could put things back on the table in separate clutches with their appropriate labels. She was feeling much better than when she had woken up. Not having to face the drive: having put an advertisement into a serious paper almost made her feel that she had sold the car already: Val had said that she might go to a film with her on Sunday afternoon if her friend didn't turn up and she didn't think he would, so that was something to look forward to, and packing china wasn't really too bad if you took it methodically and didn't expect ever to finish.

In the middle of the morning, Mr Whitehorn went out in his van to fetch the packing cases. He would be back in about an hour, he said. Meg, who had run up to the shop to hear what he said – the basement was incredibly muffled and quiet – made herself a mug of coffee and went back to work. There was a bell under the door-rug, so that she could hear it if customers came.

She was just finishing the breakfast cups when she saw it. The newspaper had gone yellow at the edges, but inside, where all the print and pictures were, it was almost as good as new. For a second, she did not pick up the page, simply stared at a large photograph of head and shoulders, and M1 MYSTERY in bold type above it.

The picture was of the girl she had picked up in Hendon. She knew that it was, before she picked it up, but she still had to do that. She *might* be wrong, but she knew she wasn't. The glasses, the hair, the rather high forehead . . . but she was smiling faintly in the picture . . .

'. . . petite, auburn-haired Mary Carmichael was found wrapped in her raincoat in a ditch in a lane not one hundred yards from the M1 north of Towcester. She had been assaulted and strangled with a lime green silk scarf that she was seen wearing when she left her office

. . . Mr Turner was discovered in the boot of the car – a black MG that police found abandoned in a car-park. The car belonged to Mr Turner, who had been stabbed a number of times and is thought to have died earlier than Miss Carmichael . . .'

She realized then that she was reading a story continued from page one. Page one of the newspaper was missing. She would never know what Mr Turner looked like. She looked again at the picture of the girl. 'Taken on holiday the previous year.' Even though she was smiling, or trying to smile, Mary Carmichael looked timid and vulnerable.

'. . . Mr Turner, a travelling salesman and owner of the car, is thought to have given a lift or lifts to Mary Carmichael and some other person, probably a man, not yet identified. The police are making extensive enquiries along the entire length of the route that Mr Turner regularly travelled. Mr Turner was married, with three children. Miss Carmichael's parents, Mr and Mrs Gerald Carmichael of Manchester, described their only daughter as very quiet and shy and without a boyfriend.'

The paper was dated March of the previous spring.

Meg found that her eyes were full of tears. Poor, poor Mary. Last year she had been an ordinary timid, not very attractive girl who had been given a lift, and then 37 been horribly murdered. How frightened she must have been before she died – with being – assaulted – and all that. And now, she was simply a desolate ghost, bound to go on trying to get lifts, or to be helped, or perhaps even to *warn* people . . . 'I'll pray for you,' she said to the picture, which now was so blurred through her tears that the smile, or attempt at one, seemed to have vanished.

She did not know how long it was before the implications, both practical and sinister, crept into her mind. But they did, and she realized that they had, because she began to shiver violently – in spite of feeling quite warm – and fright was prickling her spine up to the back of her neck.

Mystery Murders. If Mr Turner was not the murderer of Mary, then only one other person could be responsible. The horrible man. The way he had talked of almost nothing but awful murders . . . She must go to the police immediately. She could describe him down to the last detail: his clothes, his voice, his tinted spectacles, his frightful smell . . . He had been furious with her when she had put him down at the service station . . . but, one minute, before that, before *then*, when she had let him out on the shoulder where the lorry was, he had taken ages to come back into the car – had walked right round it, and then, when he got in, and she had questioned him about the girl, and described her, he had become all sweaty, and taken ages to reply to anything she said. He must have *recognized* the car! She was beginning to feel confused: there was too much to think about at once. This was where being clever would be such a help, she thought.

She began to try to think quietly, logically: absolutely nothing but lurid fragments came to mind: 'a modicum, and sometimes, let's face it, a very great deal of fear'; the girl's face as she stood under the light on the island. Meg looked back at the paper, but there was really no doubt at all. The girl in the paper *was* the same girl. So – at last she had begun to sort things out the girl *was* a ghost: the car, therefore, must be haunted. He certainly knew, or realized, something about all this: his final words – 'I'm far from sure that *I* trust *you*' – that was because she had said that she didn't trust him. So – perhaps he thought she *knew* what had happened. Perhaps he had thought she was trying to trap him, or something like that. If he *really* thought that, and he was actually guilty, he surely wouldn't leave it at that, would he? He'd be afraid of her going to the police, of what, in fact, she was shortly going to do. He couldn't *know* that she hadn't seen the girl before, in the newspaper. But if he couldn't know, how could the police?

At this point, the door-bell rang sharply, and Meg jumped. Before she could do more than leap to her feet, Mr Whitehorn's faded, kindly voice called down. 'I'm back, my dear girl. Any customers while I've been away?'

'No.' Meg ran up the stairs with relief that it was he. 'Would you like some coffee?'

'Splendid notion.' He was taking off his teddy-bear overcoat and rubbing his dry, white hands before the fan heater.

Later, when they were both nursing steaming mugs, she asked: 'Mr Whitehorn, do you remember a mystery murder case on the M1 last spring? Well, two murders really? The man was found in the boot of the car, and the girl –'

'In a ditch somewhere? Yes, indeed. All over the papers. The real trouble is, that although I adore reading detective stories, *real* detective stories, I mean, I always find real-life crime just dull. Nasty, and dull.'

'I expect you're right.'

'They caught the chap though, didn't they? I expect he's sitting in some tremendously kind prison for about eighteen months. Be out next year, I shouldn't wonder. The law seems to regard property as far more important than murder, in my opinion.'

'Who did they catch?'

'The murderer, dear, the murderer. Can't remember his name. Something like Arkwright or James. Something like that. But there's no doubt at all that they caught him. The trial was all over the papers, as well. How have you been getting on with your marathon?'

Meg found herself blushing: she explained that she had been rather idle for the last hour or so, and suggested that she make up the time by staying later. No, no, said Mr Whitehorn, such honesty should be rewarded. But, he added, before she had time to thank him, if she *did* have an hour to spend tomorrow, Saturday morning, he would be most grateful. Meg had to agree to this, but arranged to come early and leave early, because of her advertisement.

The worst of having had that apparently comforting talk with Mr Whitehorn was that if they *had* already caught the man, then there couldn't by any point in going to the police. She had no proof that she hadn't seen a picture of poor Mary Carmichael; in fact, she realized that she might easily have done so, and simply not remembered because she didn't read murder cases. Going to the police and saying that you had seen a ghost, given a ghost a *lift* in your car, and *then* seen a picture in 41 a newspaper that identified them, would just sound hysterical or mad. And there would be no point in describing the horrible man, if, in fact, he was just horrible but not a murderer. But at least she didn't have to worry about him: his behaviour had simply seemed odd and then sinister, *before* Mr Whitehorn had said that they had caught the murderer. There was nothing she needed to do about any of it. Except get rid of a haunted car.

After her scrambled egg and Mars Bar, she did some washing, including her hair and her hair-brush, and went to bed early. Just before she went to sleep, the thought occurred to her that her mother always thought that people – all people – were really better than they seemed, and her father was certain that they were worse. Possibly, they were just *what* they seemed – no more and no less.

In the morning, second post, she got a letter from her mother full of anxiety and advice. The letter, after many kind and impractical admonitions, ended: 'and you are not to think of getting up or trying to drive all this way unless you are feeling completely recovered. I do wish I could come down and look after you, but your father thinks he may be getting this wretched bug. He has read in the paper that it is all over the place, and is usually the first to get anything, as you know. Much love, darling, and take *care* of yourself.'

This made Meg feel awful about going to Mr Whitehorn's, but she had promised him, and letting down one person gave one no excuse whatsoever for letting down another. Samantha had promised to sit on the telephone while Meg was out, as she was waiting for one of her friends to call.

When she got back to the flat, Samantha was on the telephone, and Val was obviously cross with her. 'She's been *ages* talking to Bruce and she is going out with him in a minute, and I said I'd do the shopping, but she won't even say what she wants. She's a drag.'

Samantha said: 'Hold on a minute – six grapefruit and two rump steaks – that's all,' and went on listening, laughing and talking to Bruce. Meg gazed at her in dismay. How on earth were people who had read her advertisement and were *longing* to ring her up about it to get through? The trouble about Samantha was that she was so *very* marvellous to look at that it was awfully difficult to get her to do anything she didn't want to do.

Val turned kindly to Meg and said loudly; 'And your ad's in, isn't it? Samantha – you really are the limit. Meg, what would you like me to shop for you?'

Meg felt that this was terribly kind of Val, who was 43

also pretty stunning, but in a less romantic way. Neither of the girls had ever shopped for her before; perhaps Val was going to become her friend. When she had made her list of cheese, apples, milk, eggs and Nescaff, Val said, 'Look, why don't we share a small chicken? I'll buy most of it, if you'll do the cooking. For Sunday,' she added, and Meg felt that Val was almost her friend already.

Val went, and at once, Samantha said to the telephone: 'All *right*: meet you in half an hour. Bye.' In one graceful movement she was off the battered sofa and stood running her hands through her long, black hair and saying: 'I haven't got a *thing* to wear!'

'Did anyone ring for me?'

'What? Oh – yes, one person – no, two, as a matter of fact. I told them you'd be in by lunch-time.'

'Did they sound interested in the car?'

'One did. Kept asking awful technical questions I couldn't answer. The other one just wanted to know if the car could be seen at this address and the name of the owner.' She was pulling off a threadbare kimono, looking at her face in a small, magnifying mirror she seemed always to have with her. 'Another one . . .! They keep bobbling up like corks! I've gone on to this diet not a moment too soon.'

An hour went slowly by: nobody rang up about the

car. Samantha finally appeared in fantastically expensive-looking clothes as though she was about to be photographed. She borrowed 50p off Meg for a taxi and went, leaving an aura of chestnut bath-stuff all over the flat.

The weekend was a fearful anti-climax. On Saturday, three people rang up – none of them people who had called before; one said that he thought it was a drop-head, seemed, indeed, almost to accuse her of it not being, although she had distinctly said saloon in her ad. Two said they would come and look at the car: one of these actually arrived, but he only offered her a hundred pounds less than she was asking, and that was that. On Sunday morning Meg cooked for ages, the chicken and all the bits, like bread sauce and gravy, that were to live up to it. At twelve-thirty Val got a call from one of her friends, and said she was frightfully sorry, but that she had to be out to lunch after all.

'Oh dear! Shall I keep it till the evening? The chicken will be cold, but the other—'

Val interrupted her by saying with slight embarrassment that she wouldn't be back to dinner, either. '*You* eat it,' she ended, with guilty generosity.

When she had gone, the flat seemed very empty. Meg tried to comfort herself with the thought that anyway, she *couldn't* have gone to the cinema with Val, as she would have to stay in the flat in case the telephone rang. But she had been looking forward to lunch. If a person sat down to a table with you and had a meal, you stood a much better chance of getting to know them. Sundays only seemed quieter in London than they were in the country, because of the contrast of London during the week. As she sat down to her leg of chicken with bread sauce, gravy and potatoes done as her mother did them at home, she wondered whether coming to London was really much good after all. She did not seem to be making much headway: it wasn't turning out at all how she had imagined it might, and at this moment she felt rather homesick. Whatever happened, she'd go home next weekend, and talk to her mother about the whole thing. Not – the car – thing, but Careers and Life.

Two more people rang during the afternoon. One was for Samantha, but the other was about the car. They asked her whether she would drive it to Richmond for them to see it, but when she explained why she couldn't, they lost interest. She kept telling herself that it was too long a chance to risk losing other possible buyers by going out for such a long time, but as the grey afternoon settled drearily to the darker grey evening, she wondered whether she had been wrong.

She wrote a long letter to her mother, describing Samantha's clothes and Val's kindness, and saying that she was already feeling better (another lie, but how could she help it?): then she read last month's *Vogue* magazine and wondered what all the people in it, who wore rich car-coats and gave fabulous, unsimple dinner-parties and shooting lunches and seemed to know at least eight ways of doing their hair, were doing now. On the whole, they all seemed in her mind to be lying on velvet or leather sofas with one of their children in a party dress sitting quietly reading, and pots of azaleas and cyclamen round them in a room where you could only see one corner of a family portrait and a large white or honey-coloured dog at their feet on an old French carpet. She read her horoscope: it said, you will encounter some interesting people, but do not go more than half way to meet them, and watch finances – last month's horoscope anyway, so that somehow whether it had been right or not hardly counted. When she thought it must be too late for any more people to ring up, she had a long, hot bath, and tried to do her hair at least one other way. But her hair was too short, too fine, and altogether too unused to any outlandish intention, and obstinately slipped or fell back into its ordinary state. It was also the kind of uninteresting colour that 47 people never even bothered to describe in books. She yawned, a tear came out of one eye, and she decided that she had better get on with improving her mind, to which end she settled down to a vast and heavy book on Morocco that Val said people were talking about . . .

All week she packed and packed: china, glass, silver and bits of lamps and chandeliers. On Wednesday, someone rang up for her at the shop while she was out buying sausage rolls and apples for Mr Whitehorn's and her lunches. Mr Whitehorn seemed very vague about them: it hadn't seemed to be about the car, but something about her weekend plans, he thought. He *thought*, he reiterated, as though this made the whole thing more doubtful. Meg could not think who it could be – unless it was the very shy young man with red hair and a stammer who had once come in to buy a painting on glass about Nelson's death. He had been very nice, she thought, and he had stayed for quite a long time after he had bought the picture and told her about his collection of what she had learned to call Nelsoniana. That was about the only person it could be, and she hoped he'd ring again, but he didn't.

By Wednesday, she had long given up hope of anyone buying the car as a result of the advertisement. Val and

Samantha told her that Bruce and Alan both said it was the wrong time of the year to sell second-hand cars, and she decided that she had better try to sell it in the north, nearer home.

On Wednesday evening she had a sudden, irrational attack of fear. However much she reasoned with herself, she simply did not *want* to drive up the M1 alone in the car that she was now certain was haunted. She couldn't stand the thought of hearing the sounds she had heard, of seeing the girl again in the same place (possibly, why not? – ghosts were well known for repeating themselves): and when Samantha and Val came in earlier than usual and together, she had a – possibly not hopeless – idea. Would either or both of them like to come home for the weekend with her?

Their faces turned at once to each other; it was easy to see the identical appalled blankness with which they received the proposal. Before they could *say* that they wouldn't come, Meg intercepted them. 'It's lovely country, and my mother's a marvellous cook. We could go for drives in the car –' but she knew it was no good. They couldn't possibly come, they both said almost at once: they had dates, plans, it was awfully kind of her, and perhaps in the summer they might – yes, in the summer, it might be marvellous *if* there was a free weekend . . .

Afterwards, Meg sat on her bed in the very small room that she had to herself, and cried. They weren't enough her friends for her to plead with them, and if she told them why she was frightened, they would be more put off than ever.

Next morning she asked Mr Whitehorn if he had ever been up north to sales and auctions and things like that.

Yes, he went from time to time.

'I suppose you wouldn't like to come up this weekend to stay? I could drive you to any places you wanted to go.'

Mr Whitehorn looked at her with his usual tired face, but also with what she could see was utter amazement.

'My dear child,' he said, when he had had time to think of it, 'I couldn't possibly do anything, *anything* at all like that at such short notice. It would throw out all my plans, you see. I always make plans for the weekend. Perhaps you have not realized it,' he went on, 'but I am a homosexual, you see. I thought you would know; running this shop and the states I get into. But I *always* plan my free time. I am lunching with a very dear friend in Ascot, and sometimes, not always, I stay the night there.' The confidence turned him pink. 'I had absolutely no intention of *misleading* you.'

Meg said of course not, and then they both apologized to each other and said it didn't matter in the least.

On Thursday evening both girls were out, and Meg, who had not slept at all well for the last two nights, decided that she was too tired to go on her own to the cinema, although it was *A Man for All Seasons* that she had missed and always wanted to see. She ate a poached egg and half a grapefruit that Samantha said was left over from her diet, and suddenly she had a brain-wave. What she was frightened of, she told herself, was the idea that the poor girl would be waiting for her again at Hendon. If, therefore, she *avoided* Hendon, and got on to the M1 further north, she would be free of this anxiety. There might still be those awful sounds again, like she had heard the first time, but she would just have to face that, drive steadily home, and when she got there, she decided, she would jolly well tell her mother about the whole thing. The idea, and the decision to tell her mother, cheered her so much that she felt less tired, and went down to the car to fetch the map. There, the car rug that her mother had given her in case she did not have enough on her bed pricked her conscience. She had managed to toil up the stairs with the flowers and marmalade and her case, but she had completely forgotten the rug; this was probably because her mother had put it in the car herself, and it now lay on the floor in the back. She would take it home, as she really didn't need it, and usually her father used it to protect his legs from draughts when he sat in or out of doors.

She found a good way on the map. She simply did not go left on to Hendon Way, but used the A1000 through Barnet and turned left on to the St Albans road. She could get on to the M1 on the way to Watford. It was easy. That evening she packed her party dress so that her mother could see it. She always packed the night before, so that she didn't rush too much in the mornings, got to work on time, and parked her car, as usual, round the corner from the shop. Mr Whitehorn had simply chalked 'No Parking' on the brick wall, and so far it had always worked.

On Friday morning, she and Mr Whitehorn met each other elaborately, as though far more had occurred between them than had actually happened: the first half hour was heavy with off-handed good will, and they seemed to get in each other's way far more often than usual. They used the weather as a kind of demilitarized zone of conversation. Mr Whitehorn said that he heard on the wireless that there was going to be fog again, and Meg, who had heard it too, said oh dear and thanked him for telling her. Later in the morning, when things had eased between them, Mr Whitehorn asked her whether she had been successful in selling her car. Trains were so much easier in this weather, he added. They were, indeed. But she could hardly tell him that as she lived seventeen miles from the station, and her parents didn't drive, and the last bus had left by the time the train she would be able to catch had arrived, and her salary certainly couldn't afford a taxi . . . she couldn't tell him any of that: it would look like asking, begging for more money – she would never do it . . .

But the train became a recurrent temptation throughout the long cold and, by the afternoon, foggy day. She banished the idea in the end by reminding herself that, with the cost of the advertisement, she simply did not have the money for the train fare: the train was out of the question.

Mr Whitehorn, who had spent the morning typing lists for the Customs (he typed with three fingers in erratic, irritable bursts), said that he would buy their lunch, as he needed the exercise.

When he had gone, Meg, who had been addressing labels to be stuck on to the packing cases, felt so cold that she fetched the other paraffin heater from the basement and lit it upstairs. She did not like to get another cardigan from her case in the car, as in spite of its being so near, it was out of sight from the shop, and Mr Whitehorn hated the shop to be left empty for a moment. This made her worry, stupidly, whether she had locked the car. It was the kind of worry that one had like wondering if one had actually posted a letter *into* the letter-box: of course, one would have, but once any idea to the contrary set in, it would not go. So the moment he came back with hot sausages and Smith's crisps from the pub, she rushed out to the car. She had, in fact, left one back door open: she could have sworn that she hadn't but there it was. She got herself another cardigan out of her case in the boot, and returned to her lunch. It was horrible out; almost dark, or at any rate opaque, with the fog, and the bitter, acrid air that seemed to accompany fogs in towns. At home, it would be a thick white mist – well, nearly white, but certainly not smelling as this fog smelled. The shop, in contrast, seemed quite cosy. One or two people came to 'look around' while they ate; but there was never very much to see. Mr Whitehorn put all the rubbish that got included in lots he had bid for on to trays with a mark saying that anything on the tray cost 50p, or £1. Their serious stuff nearly always seemed to go abroad, or to another dealer. Mr Whitehorn always made weak but kindly little jokes about his rubbish collectors, as he called the ones who bought old photograph albums, moulded glass vases, or hair-combs made of tortoise-shell and bits of broken paste.

While she was making their coffee, Meg wondered whether perhaps Mr Whitehorn would be a good person to talk about the haunted car to. Obviously, asking him to stay had been a silly mistake. But he might be just the person to understand what was worrying her; to believe her and to let her talk about it. That was what she most wanted, she realized. Someone, almost anyone, to *talk* to her about it: to sort out what was honestly frightening, and what she had imagined or invented as fright.

But immediately after lunch, he set about his typing again, and got more and more peevish, crumpling up bits of paper and throwing them just outside the wastepaper basket, until she hardly liked to ask him, at five, whether she might go.

However, she did ask, and he said it would be all right.

He could not know how difficult she found it to leave: she said good night to him twice by mistake, started to put her old tweed coat on, and then decided that with the second cardigan she wouldn't need it, took ages tying on her blue silk head-square, and nearly forgot her bag. She took out her car keys while she could find them easily in the light, shut the shop door behind her and, after one more look at him, angrily crouched over his typewriter, went to the car.

Once she got into the car, her courage and common sense returned. It was only, at the worst, a four-hour journey: she would be home then, and everything would be all right. She flung her overcoat into the back – it was far easier to drive without it hanging round the gear lever – had one final look at her map before she shut the car door, and set off.

It was more interesting going a different way out of London, even though it seemed to be slower, but the traffic, the fog, and making sure all the time that she was on the right road, occupied her mind, almost to the exclusion of anything else. She found her way on to the M1 quite easily; the signs posting it were more frequent and bigger than any other sign.

She drove for over an hour on the motorway, and there was no sound in the car, no agonized, laboured breathing – nothing. It was getting rather hot, but the heater cleared the windscreen and she couldn't do without it for long. The fog was better, too, although patchy, and in the clearer bits she could see the fine, misty rain that was falling all the time. She was sticking to the left-hand lane, because although it meant that lorries passed her from time to time, she felt safer in the fog than if she had been in the middle, and possibly unable to see either side of the road. She opened a crack of window because the car seemed to be getting impossibly hot and full of stale air. Another two hours, she thought, and decided that she might as well stop to take off her thick cardigan – she could use the hard shoulder just for that – and perhaps she had made far too much of her nerves and anxiety about the whole journey. She drew up carefully, then saw a service area ahead – safer in one of those. 'At least I didn't give in,' she thought, and thought also how ashamed of herself she would have been if she had.

As she drew up in the car-park, she was just about to get out of her cardigan, when a huge hand reached out in front of her and twitched the driving mirror so that she could see him. He was smiling, his eyes full of triumph and malice. His breath reeked over her shoulder as she gave a convulsive gasp of pure shock. 'You must be a ghost!' She heard herself repeating this in a high voice utterly unlike her own. 'You must be a ghost: you *must* be!'

'Only had to pick the car lock twice. You shouldn't have locked it *again* in the middle of the day.'

She knew she should start the car and drive back out

on to the road, but she couldn't see behind her, and nearly lost all control when she felt something hard and pointed sticking into the back of her neck.

'They caught Mr Wrong, you see. But you seemed to know *so much*, and as you were driving the same car, I simply had to catch up with you somehow. Two birds with one stone, as it were.'

She made an attempt to get the brake off, but a hand clamped over her wrist with such sudden force that she cried out.

'Ever since you turned me out in that unkind manner, I have been trying to track you down. That is all I have done, but your advertisement was a great help.' She saw him watching her face in the mirror and licking the scum off his lips. She made a last effort.

'I shall turn you out again – any minute – I shall!'

He sucked in his breath, but he was still smiling.

'Oh no, you won't. This time, it will all be done my way.'

She thought she screamed once, in that single second of astonished disbelief and denial before she felt the knife jab smoothly through the skin on her neck when speechless terror overwhelmed her and she became nothing but fear – heart thudding, risen in her throat as though it would burst from her: she put one hand to the

wound and felt no knife – only her own blood – there, as
he said:

'Don't worry *too* much: just stick to fear. The fate
worse than death tends to occur after it. I've always
liked them warm.'

A Note on Elizabeth Jane Howard

Born in 1923, Elizabeth Jane Howard was awarded the John Llewellyn Rhys Memorial Prize for her book *The Beautiful Visit*. Her subsequent novels were *The Long View*, *The Sea Change*, *After Julius*, *Odd Girl Out*, *Something in Disguise*, and *Getting it Right*. She has also written fourteen television scripts, a biography of Bettina von Arnim with Arthur Helps, a cookery book with Fay Maschler, two film scripts, and has edited two anthologies and published a book of ghost stories. *The Light Years*, the first volume of Elizabeth Jane Howard's acclaimed and bestselling quartet of novels, The Cazalet Chronicle, was published in 1990. This was followed by *Marking Time* (1991), *Confusion* (1993) and *Casting Off* (1995).

Other titles in this series